D0229518

EGMONT
We bring stories to life

First published in Great Britain 2012 by Dean,
an imprint of Egmont UK Limited
239 Kensington High Street, London W8 6SA
All rights reserved.

© 2012 Prism Art & Design Limited, a HIT Entertainment company.
Based on an original idea by D. Gingell, D. Jones and characters created by R. J. M. Lee.
The Fireman Sam name and character are trademarks of Prism Art & Design Limited,
a HIT Entertainment company.

HiT entertainment

ISBN 978 0 6035 6676 9
51288/1
Printed in China

King of the Jungle

One hot summer's day, Station Officer Steele was talking to Sam and Elvis about how things can burst into flames all by themselves.

"In this hot weather it can happen to haystacks," he explained. "One of the warning signs is if the hay smells like toffee."

"I could eat a giant toffee right now," said Elvis, licking his lips.

Station Officer Steele sighed and continued with his fire safety talk.

In the village, Norman was pretending to be Tarzan. "Aaa-eee-aaa-eee-aaa!" he yelled.

James and Sarah called to him across the street, but Norman ignored them at first.

"Who are you shouting at? Me not Norman. Me Narzan, King of the Jungle," he said.

Mandy arrived and asked Norman if his mum knew he was wearing her bath mat.

"Me not got mam. Me live with gorillas," he said.

Norman greedily ate a banana from outside Dilys' shop and threw the skin over his shoulder.

But Trevor was just delivering some fruit to the shop. He slipped on the skin, landing on the floor!

"Oops, sorry, Trevor," said Norman.

"Norman Price, I've seen better behaved chimps than you!" said Trevor.

"We're going to play knights and you're not invited!" said James, avoiding the fallen fruit.

"Me Narzan. Me go to jungle," replied Norman.

Later on, James and Sarah were playing in the fields.

"We are brave knights and with our trusty swords, we will attack the castle of evil Baron Blackheart," said James, pointing at a stack of hay bales.

The twins fought the scarecrow and threw it to the ground. Then they both sniffed the air.

"Toffee!" said James, taking a bag of sweets from his pocket. "That smell must be these. Want one?"

The twins didn't see that wisps of smoke were coming from the top of the haystack!

At the Fire Station, Fireman Sam was showing Elvis his new invention.

"You stick the broom handle into haystacks and the thermometer on the end tells you how hot they are," explained Sam.

Elvis stuck a broom handle straight into his pile of pasta.

"Cor, my spaghetti's hot stuff!" said Elvis.

"It should do the trick on the local haystacks," said Fireman Sam. "Station Officer Steele wants us to check them all."

In the fields, Norman was trying to get Dusty and Woolly to play jungle animals, but they just wanted to chase their own tails!

Suddenly, Dusty stopped and sniffed. "Woof!"

"You smell trouble?" said Norman, sniffing the air. "Me do too!"

He looked around and saw the twins playing near the smoking haystack.

"Oh no! Fire! Get away from the haystack!" yelled Norman, jumping up and down, waving his arms.

James saw Norman in the distance.

"Look, he's waving at us," James said to Sarah.

"The haystack is on fire!" shouted Norman.

"I think he's shouting something, but I can't hear him," said James.

The twins decided to ignore Norman and get back to building a moat around the haystack.

Norman had tried to warn them. He must now get help, so raced off to raise the alarm!

At the Fire Station, Fireman Sam picked up the emergency message.

"Great Fires of London! We've got a hot haystack on our hands!" said Sam.

Quick as a flash, Fireman Sam and Elvis put on their helmets and jumped aboard Jupiter.

The blue lights flashed and the siren wailed, as Jupiter raced along the country roads. Penny followed closely behind in Venus.

Nee Nah! Nee Nah!

The twins were still building their moat when bits of burning hay began to fall around them.

"Oh no!" cried James.

Sarah and James started to run away, but James tripped over his sword and fell on the ground.

"I've twisted my ankle!" he cried.

Sarah dragged him away from the haystack.

Nee Nah! Nee Nah!

The twins could hear Jupiter approaching.

The fire engine came racing through the field.

"Uncle Sam!" cried James.

"Hang on, kids. Here I come!" said Fireman Sam. He snatched them to safety, just as some burning hay landed where they'd been standing.

Penny and Elvis hosed down the flames until the fire was out.

"That was a close thing!" said Sam, as he put his arms around the twins.

Penny and Elvis stepped away from the haystack and Fireman Sam picked up his new invention.

"Right, let's take your temperature," he said, pushing the broom handle into the haystack.

He waited a few minutes and then pulled the handle out and looked at the thermometer.

"Perfect! This haystack is as cool as a cucumber, so there's no more danger," said Sam.

The Fire Crew packed their equipment away and took James and Sarah home.

That evening, everyone was in Bella's café.

"Remember, it can be dangerous to play near haystacks at this time of the year," said Sam. "You should thank Norman for raising the alarm."

"Thanks, Norman!" said James. "Sorry – thanks, Narzan!"

"Aaa-eee-aaa-eee-aaa!" cried Norman.

And James cried, "Aaa-eee-aaa-eee-aaa!" as Fireman Sam stuck his fingers in his ears!